Bella the goose lived at the bottom of an untidy garden.

Every day she was given a plate of scraps and a bowl of water.

Little birds came and talked to her, but Bella was unhappy.

# Bella Goes to Sea

## BENEDICT BLATHWAYT

*For Alice, and Elizabeth Rose*

First published in 2017 by
BC Books,
an imprint of
Birlinn Limited
West Newington House
10 Newington Road
Edinburgh EH9 1QS

*www.bcbooksforkids.co.uk*

in association with
Tackle & Books
6–8 Main Street
Tobermory
Isle of Mull PA75 6NU

*www.tackleandbooks.co.uk*

Parts of this book first appeared in
*Bella's Big Adventure* and *Bella Goes to Sea*, published
by Random House Children's Books, 1996

ISBN: 978 1 78027 457 7

British Library Cataloguing-in-Publication Data
A catalogue record for this book is available
from the British Library

Designed by Mark Blackadder

Printed and bound by Livonia, Latvia

One night a strong wind blew the roof off Bella's shed.

'Fly away! Fly away!' sang the little birds.

Bella had never learned to fly, but she scrambled out of her shed.
This was her chance to be free!

Bella went into town. It was very busy and noisy.
I don't belong here, thought Bella.

The dogs in the park chased her.
I don't belong here, thought Bella.

She dived into the canal to escape . . .

. . . but the ducks and swans did not want her on their stretch of water.
I don't belong here, thought Bella.

Bella swam away from the town and on into the country.
The farm animals had never seen a goose before.
'Perhaps you belong at sea,' they said. 'Keep going!'

So Bella kept paddling, and the river grew wider . . .

. . . and wider . . .

. . . until it reached the sea.

Now I am lost, thought Bella.
She was tired and hungry.

A fishing boat came over the horizon.
Bella flapped her wings and honked loudly.

'Hello!' said Robbie the fisherman. 'What are you doing so far out at sea?
You don't belong here.' He grabbed Bella and took her on board.

When he returned to the harbour, Robbie led Bella up the hill to his little house. 'You can stay with me,' he said.

Robbie let Bella sleep in the garden shed.
She couldn't believe how lucky she was.

Sometimes Robbie took Bella down to the harbour café,
and bought her a milkshake and biscuits as a treat.

But whenever Robbie went to sea, Bella had to stay behind.
'You can guard the house,' he said.

Bella was lonely when Robbie was away.
She wished her wings were stronger so that she could fly after him.

I *will* learn to fly, thought Bella. She tried and tried and tried . . .
and at last she was flying perfectly.

One morning Bella followed Robbie down to the harbour…

…and on, out to sea.

She landed on the boat. Robbie was cross. 'A fishing boat is no place for a goose,' he said, but he let her stay.

Bella loved being at sea.

That afternoon the sky grew dark and a wild wind began to blow.

It was much too rough for fishing, and then the engine broke down.

The little boat was blown onto the rocks with a great crunch.

'We are shipwrecked,' said Robbie. 'Somebody will come and help us.'

But nobody came. Nobody knew they were there.

The next morning Robbie wrote a message and tied it to Bella's leg.

'Get help!' he said. 'Fly away home!'
I can do that, thought Bella.

Bella flew straight to the harbour café.
The fishermen read the message tied to Bella's leg.

They set out at once to rescue Robbie.

'Brave Bella!' said Robbie. 'I will build a new fishing boat
and you can come with me whenever I go to sea.'

Bella was so happy.